MAKING

THE

GRADE

BAYVIEW HIGH

MAKING
THE
GRADE

H.G. Sotzek

Vanwell Publishing Limited
St. Catharines, Ontario

Vanwell Publishing acknowledges the financial support of the
Government of Canada through the Book Publishing Industry
Development Program for our publishing activities.

Vanwell Publishing acknowledges the Government of Ontario
through the Ontario Media Development Corporation's Book
Initiative.

Vanwell Publishing Limited   **In the United States**
P.O. Box 2131   P.O. Box 1207
1 Northrup Crescent   Lewiston, NY
St. Catharines, ON   USA 14092
Canada L2R 7S2
sales@vanwell.com
1-800-661-6136

Produced and designed by Tea Leaf Press Inc.
www.tealeafpress.com

Printed in Canada

National Library of Canada Cataloguing in Publication

Sotzek, Hannelore
     Making the grade / H.G. Sotzek.

(Bayview High, ISSN 1702-0174)
ISBN 1-55068-095-1

     I. Title. II. Series.

PS8587.O85M34 2003   jC813'.6   C2003-901080-5
PZ7

For Mike Hough,
who had the courage to follow his heart.
May his humor and spirit live on.

chapter 1

the life of Riley

A hush came over the busy restaurant. Bodies were frozen in place. Pieces of soft white paper floated to the floor. Then it happened again.

"WOO HOO!" Riley Jackson yelled for the second time. "I AM BACK!" He was standing in the aisle. Both of his arms were raised in the air. Paper napkins were now scattered around him on the worn tile floor.

Everyone was staring at Riley. The only person not staring was Lulu Fontaine. She rolled her eyes and sipped her chocolate milk shake.

Riley grinned playfully at his main rival for top grades as she ignored him. "Don't you have anything to say?" he said. Riley leaned over the top of her wooden booth. "Are you ignoring me because I'm going to be number one again?"

Lulu looked up at him and put on her sunglasses. She gathered her books and leather bag and calmly walked away. She paused in the aisle for a moment and then kept right on going. Lulu pushed open the heavy glass door and walked into the September sunlight.

The clatter of dishes and clinking of glasses filled the room again. Riley's voice now faded into the noise of Lee's Restaurant. The food servers called out orders to the kitchen.

Riley ran his fingers through his thick, blond hair and fell back into his own booth. He gave a broad, glowing smile. Today was the first day of his last year at Bayview High. This was going to be *his* year. It had taken a lot of hard work to stay on top. Next year he was off to university. He was going to be very important in the business world. Everything was all planned out. His parents were making sure of it.

"It's a good thing that you don't like to make a scene!" Tyson Richards said with a grin. He was already spread out in the booth. His long arms were stretched across the back of the wooden seat. Tyson shook his head, smiling. "It's a good thing that Lulu can take a joke."

"Good old Lulu. I'm surprised that she didn't give me one of her classic comeback comments. Maybe she was appreciating how great I really am," Riley laughed. "Ah, it's good to be the king!" he said. Riley picked up an onion ring and popped it into his mouth.

"Ah, you should be thanking *me*, your highness," Tyson said.

"Thanking *you?*" said Riley.

"That's right. You do so well because I inspire you!" Tyson said, as he pointed to himself. A playful grin spread across his face.

"Please!" Riley said. He waved him away with his hand.

Now Tyson was laughing. He threw an onion ring at Riley. Riley tried to duck but got hit in the forehead. He leaned across the table to give Tyson a jab on the arm. Tyson raised his right eyebrow, and Riley stopped in his tracks.

Riley looked up and saw Beth Sanchez come down the aisle. Her long, dark ponytail swung from side to side as she walked. He slid over to make room for her.

Riley and Tyson had known Beth since grade five. They had met her by accident. Riley had just pitched his famous fastball during a baseball game. Like always, Tyson struck it hard. The ball flew across the schoolyard. It was going straight for the principal's shiny gold sports car. The boys could only watch it whiz through the air and wait for the crash. The next thing they knew, someone jumped up and made a dive for the ball. Beth caught it with her bare hands! For once, Riley and Tyson were speechless. Beth became their hero. She never let them forget it either.

"Beth, my love, where have you been all my life?" Riley sang.

Beth glanced at Riley with his arms wide open. She pretended to ignore him.

"What's with Riley?" Beth said to Tyson. She sat down and plopped her keys on the table. Beth rarely carried a purse. She usually stuffed things in the pocket of her jean jacket. "If it doesn't fit, then I don't need it," she often said.

"He's the 'king of the world,'" Tyson said.

"I don't remember crowning him," she laughed. "I guess it's better than the 'Mr. Wonderful' stage he went through."

"True. Or the 'Master of the Universe' thing last year," Tyson said.

"You people just don't appreciate the magic that is *me*," Riley said. Then he winked. Riley leaned happily into the corner of the booth. He loved to hang out with Tyson and Beth. He really liked being with people who understood his sense of humor. He knew that some people thought he could be a bit of a clown. Not Tyson and Beth, though. They *got* it.

Beth rolled her eyes and grinned. "Hey, what did you guys think about the timetable change? What course are you in now?"

Tyson looked puzzled. "What are you talking about?" he said.

"The advanced debating course was cancelled at the last minute," she said. "I found out at registration this morning. People who were signed up for it have been moved into other courses instead. I'm in photography now," Beth said. She pulled a piece of paper from her pocket. "The new class starts tomorrow."

Tyson read over the notice about the change. "Oh," said Tyson. "I didn't hear about that. Then again, I wasn't signed up for debating. Weren't you supposed to be in that course, Riley? Did they put you into photography, too?"

The smile drained away from Riley's face. "Yes, but I'll have to do something about it. There's no way I can take *photography*."

"What's the problem?" Beth asked. "You'll ace it like you do everything else."

"I'm not worried about the grade. I'm worried about my parents," Riley said. "I'm supposed to take debating. It will really help me out in my career. Plus it will look good on my university applications." He pushed aside the onion rings. "My parents will not like this change at all. I am doomed." Riley leaned his head on his hand.

Beth and Tyson exchanged looks.

Riley's parents were lawyers. They had built up their own law firm. They worked long hours all day and then came home and worked some more. Mr. and Mrs. Jackson demanded the same from Riley. They expected him to be perfect. They wanted nothing but the best.

Beth reached out and put her hand on Riley's shoulder. "Don't worry about it," she said. "You never know, they may even like the course change. Maybe it will be okay."

Riley knew she was only trying to cheer him up. "Thanks, Beth, but this is a losing battle. I'm supposed to take debating. A new course is *not* acceptable!" he said.

"Whoa! Did you just say that it's 'not acceptable?'" Tyson leaned back and studied Riley. "You're starting to sound like your parents. You need to relax. Beth is right. Photography is okay. I took it last year. Remember? The teacher is picky, but the class was good. Why don't you come over to my house after school? I'll show you my photographs. *They* should inspire you!"

"Well, maybe," Riley answered. "Are you coming too, Beth?"

"No. I've got to get to work soon," Beth said.

"I thought you only worked on weekends," Tyson said.

"That's my job at the variety store. I just got a second job at the public library. I'll be stocking books to help pay for university next year," Beth explained. "It looks like you won't be seeing much of me this term." Beth's father had lost his job last year. Now she always seemed strapped for cash.

"Well, don't work too hard. Maybe we can pencil in some time with you before winter break!" Riley teased.

"Thanks a lot!" Beth said, and she threw an onion ring his way.

chapter 2

keeping the peace

The Richards' home was like a battle scene. Tyson's younger brothers, Jamal and Darnell, were crouched on the floor. They were picking up pieces of broken glass and bent metal. The pile used to be their mother's favorite reading lamp. The boys did not look happy.

Tyson stepped around the mess. He waved hello to his mother. Mrs. Richards was standing overtop of her sons. Tyson's mom never had to raise her voice when she was angry. She had a fierce look that would turn anybody to stone. When she gave it, her kids froze.

"What happened?" Tyson asked. Then he noticed Jamal's football lying in the corner of the room. "Aha! You guys were tossing the football in the house *again*." Tyson said. Then he turned to Riley. "Let's go upstairs where life is calm, cool, and collected," he said.

"At least it's never dull around here!" Riley said. He followed Tyson to his room.

Riley sat down on his favorite chair in Tyson's room. It was soft black leather. He leaned back and sighed. Tyson pulled a thick black binder from his bookcase and handed it to him. Riley flipped through his photographs.

Tyson turned on his stereo and sounds of jazz filled the room. "*Ahhh*. That's much better," Tyson said. He dropped on the bed and put his hands behind his head. "Now *this* is music!" He closed his eyes.

"Not more jazz!" Riley groaned as a trumpet rang from Tyson's speakers. "Who listens to jazz in high school?"

"Riley, you may be gifted in the classroom. You just don't know how to appreciate the finer things in life. And jazz is the *finest*."

"But it makes no sense!" Riley said.

"If I have to explain it to you..." Tyson trailed off. He closed his eyes again and moved his head to the music. Riley went back to Tyson's photographs.

Two jazz CDs later, Riley was still frowning.

Tyson opened his eyes. "Relax, Riley. Are you still worried about your parents?

Photography is only one class. What's it going to hurt if you take a few pictures? It's not as though *you* switched classes—the school did. Besides, your parents have to learn that they can't rule your life forever. Right?"

"No, of course not. You're right. Not forever," Riley said. *Forever? I hope not*, he thought to himself.

"I'd say today went pretty well for the first day back. Hey, did I tell you the latest about that guy at Lincoln High? He was charged by the police for those stolen exam papers."

"Really? I only heard that someone was kicked out of summer school. I didn't know he was stealing stuff," said Riley.

"Oh, yeah!" Tyson said. "The guy sold copies of the exams he stole. Over a dozen students were caught buying them. The guy made a huge profit—until he was caught."

"Are you sure? It sounds like a rumor to me," Riley replied.

"No! It's true. My dad told me," Tyson said. He loved to brag about his father. Mr. Richards was a sergeant on the city police force.

"Well, I guess it doesn't surprise me. The guys at Lincoln have been doing this kind of stupid stuff for years. It's time they got caught. They deserve it," Riley said.

Tyson shook his head. "My dad said that the Lincoln principal was blown away. Some of the students were already getting 'A's.' It was a huge surprise."

Riley looked doubtful. "If they were that smart, then why would they do something risky like that?"

Tyson shrugged. "I don't know. I guess it depends on how desperate you can get."

Then Tyson sat up on the edge of the bed. He looked over his right shoulder and then over his left. Riley looked around, too. No one was there. Tyson leaned toward Riley and waved him closer. "I have a feeling that something is going to go down at Bayview, too," Tyson said. "I've heard that some of the teachers have their eye out this year."

"No one at Bayview would be crazy enough to buy or sell exams," Riley said. Then he noticed a long, low rumble in his stomach. Riley looked at the time. "I can't believe how late it is!" Riley said. "Sorry, Tyson, but I'd better get going. I'm starving. Besides, I want to do some research for next year."

"What? School has barely started *this year*. I think your parents are the least of your worries!" Tyson said, laughing.

chapter 3

sic 'em, Stinky

Riley pulled into his driveway just past six o'clock. The large gray stone house at the end of Westmount Drive looked deserted. His silver sports car was the only car there. *It must be another late night at the office for Mom and Dad,* he thought. The house was completely quiet as he stepped inside. Riley dropped his backpack on the hardwood floor. The sound echoed though the front hallway.

A moment later, the sound of paws galloping down the stairs filled the silence. Stinky, the family dog, was doing her usual "meet and greet." In an instant she was airborne and leaping at Riley. Before he knew it, Riley was knocked backward and pinned to the ground. The bull terrier wagged her tail excitedly. She almost seemed to be grinning. Loose bits of fur flew in the air around them.

"STINKY! GET OFF ME!" Riley yelled and heaved the massive dog off his chest. Riley secretly loved being greeted by her. It felt good just to have another body in the house when he came home.

A red flashing light on the telephone caught his eye. "Ah, messages!" Riley said. He went over to the phone. Stinky trotted behind him.

"You have five messages," the machine said. Tyson had called, reminding him to relax. Then Beth asked for a ride to school the next day. The other messages were from his parents.

Riley had a strange relationship with his mom and dad. They "talked" through messages these days. It was rare if they had an actual conversation.

Beep beep beep. "Riley?" his mother's voice said. "Listen, honey, we won't be home late tonight. We're almost done at the office. I've just got to finish working on this file. I think I'll make a real home-cooked dinner tonight. We'll see you soon." *Click.* Riley checked the time of the message. She had called at five o'clock.

Beep beep beep. "Hello. It's Mom again. It's almost six o'clock. Dad and I have finally left the office and are on our way home. First we have to stop at the courthouse. We shouldn't be long. I think we'll pick up some dinner for you on the way home. Bye, honey!" *Click.*

Beep beep beep. "Riley? It's your father. It's six-thirty, and we're still at the courthouse. There seems to be some sort of hold-up with our paperwork. Thankfully, your mother is on top of it. We may be longer than we hoped, though." *Muffled voices in the background.* "That was your mother. She said that you should just go ahead and eat without us. Have the leftover pizza in the fridge. Bye, Son." *Click.*

Riley shook his head. "I could have told them they would be late. Well, at least there's pizza! Come on, Stink Bomb," Riley said.

He searched through the boxes of takeout food in the fridge. "Aha!" Riley said. He pulled out his parents' pizza from the night before. His hopes fell when he opened the box. *"Ugh.* Anchovies! Nasty." Riley began to peel off the toppings. "I hope you like fish," he said as he tossed the toppings to the dog.

Riley munched on his pizza on the way to his room. Stinky was close behind him. She took a flying leap and landed on the middle of Riley's bed. The white dog lay her head over her front legs. She spent the next few hours watching Riley surf the Internet. Riley was going to get into the best business program next year. No matter what. It was never too early to check out good schools.

Graduating year, he thought. He smiled when he thought of one of his parents' favorite lines. "It's the doorway to my future." It was cheesy but true.

Riley checked the time on his computer. It was ten o'clock. Just then, keys jangled in the front door. Stinky perked up and raced down the stairs.

"STINKY! GET OFF ME!" Riley heard his father yell.

A knot began to grow in Riley's stomach. He did not know how he was going to explain his new class timetable.

Riley did not even hear his mother come up the stairs. He jumped when he saw her standing in the doorway. Even at the end of a long business day, his mother still looked perfect. Not a hair of her chin-length, wavy blond hair was out of place. Riley's father always said that Riley got his mother's good looks.

"Hello, darling! Oh, good. You are studying. Did you eat? I am sorry about dinner. We just could not get away sooner. This new case will be very important for our firm. We have to take extra care with it," Erika Jackson said.

"You understand, don't you honey?" Riley recognized the tone in her voice. The last part really was not a question.

Mr. Jackson poked his head into Riley's room. "How was your first day back?" his father asked. He was loosening his gray silk tie. The jacket of his dark blue Italian suit was draped over his arm.

"Not bad. Except for one *small* change of plans," Riley said. He winced at the mention of the news he was about to give.

Mrs. Jackson noticed the worried look on Riley's face. "Riley, what is it? You know you can talk to us."

Riley took a deep breath and then blurted out his news. "The school office changed my class timetable." He closed his eyes tightly and waited. His parents stood at his door staring at him. He had their full attention now. Riley pulled out the letter from the school and thrust it into his father's hands.

His father frowned as he read it. "This is out of the question. Tomorrow you will go to the office and explain that you need to take the debating course. Even if you have to do it after school. You need this course for your future. Do you understand, Son?"

Riley nodded slowly.

His mother kissed him on the forehead. "Good! I know it may sound harsh, but your father is right. You need to focus on what is best for your future," she said. Then the partners of Jackson & Jackson left his room.

"Great," Riley said as he hung his head. "Just great." He could feel the knot in his stomach growing bigger. Now there was tightness in his chest, too.

chapter 4

just point and shoot

The guidance office was no help at all. There was no debating course at all this year—not even at another school.

Mrs. Haskins gave him one final piece of advice before he left. "High grades are important, Riley. You also need to take a variety of subjects. I see that you have not taken any art courses yet. The photography course should be a good fit for you," she said. That was the end of the discussion.

Riley stormed out of her office and into the busy hallway. Things seemed more hectic during the first week of school. Riley found himself caught in a crowd of people on their way to class. As he pushed through the group, he bumped hard into someone.

"Hey!" the student exclaimed. Riley had knocked her to the floor.

Riley looked down and saw a girl in a vintage brown suede jacket. She adjusted her denim skirt as she stood up. Her long, wavy hair tumbled over her shoulders.

"Oh, sorry," he said. Riley found himself talking to Willow Thomson.

Willow Thomson was tall—almost six feet tall. Her long, lean legs seemed to make up most of her. The rest of her was flat-out beautiful, too. She had long dark lashes and soft red lips. Her thick, wavy hair looked silky.

It was no wonder that Willow had been modeling since grade nine. It was also no wonder that she was alone when Riley bumped into her. Willow did not hang around any of the girls in her class. They all seemed to think she was a snob. No guy would ever dream of asking her out. Who would want to risk getting rejected by a model?

"You should watch where you're going," Willow said. She pushed a stray lock of hair out of her face. She stood eye to eye with him.

Bumping into Willow was as much contact as Riley had ever had with her. He had no idea what to say. The words were stuck between his brain and his throat. "Um…right…well…at least I hope you had a good 'trip'! Maybe I'll see you next 'fall'?" he joked, trying to act cool. *What am I saying?* he said to himself.

Willow stared at him as though he had another head growing out of his neck. She tossed her hair over her shoulder and continued on her way.

"Geez! Beautiful women have no sense of humor," he said. Riley turned and went in the opposite direction.

"What's that? Did you say I don't have a sense of humor?" a friendly voice said. Beth had fallen in step beside him.

Beth was friendly, funny, and casual. She seemed to be the complete opposite of Willow. For one thing, she was about a foot shorter than Willow. She was a lot friendlier-looking too. Beth had on yet another pair of faded jeans. Today her handmade sweater was soft pink. Her dark hair was pulled back again into a long ponytail. It flipped up at her shoulders.

"Oh! Hi, Beth," Riley said. "No, no. I meant Willow. I bumped into her by accident. I tried to make a joke about it to smooth things over. She just looked at me like I was a freak."

"Willow Thomson? Well, she may not be the friendliest girl in school. I wouldn't say that she doesn't have a sense of humor, though. Have you considered that your joke wasn't funny?" Beth asked.

"Are you kidding?" he said. "I have a great sense of humor!"

"Riley, I have been listening to your 'jokes' for ages. I'm sorry to tell you that you are no comedian. By the way, are you going to be joining me in photography today?" she said.

Riley grew serious. "It looks like it. I don't seem to have much of a choice right now."

"Look at it this way. You will be starting off your morning with your favorite person—me!" Beth said.

Riley flashed a smile and rolled his deep blue eyes. Then the two of them made their way down to the photography lab. The room was already filled with students when they arrived. Riley looked around. Most of the people had cameras. Some were pocket-sized. Riley saw a few cameras with large lenses. They looked like the kind that professional photographers used. A few students had equipment that must have been as old as their parents.

Riley had never had Mr. Williams for a teacher before. He had never even met him. In fact, Riley had only really *heard* Mr. Williams. The teacher had a booming voice and deep laugh that rose above the noise. Sometimes

Riley passed him in the halls. He always noticed the *zhe-zhe-zhe* sound the teacher's brown corduroy pants made. His worn leather dress shoes squeaked when he walked, too.

Mr. Williams was known at Bayview for his sense of style—or lack of it. Students would try to guess which of his two sweaters he would be wearing. It might be his orange-and-brown checked vest one day. He could be wearing his bright green sweater vest instead. Mr. Williams did not look like a photography teacher.

Riley just did not get it. *Aren't all artists supposed to wear black?* he thought.

The teacher smiled and said, "Good morning! Welcome to photography! There are some new additions to my class list, I see." He nodded at Riley and Beth. Mr. Williams pulled out a pencil tucked behind his ear. He made a small check with it on his class attendance sheet.

Then Mr. Williams held up a camera with a long lens. "This is a Single Lens Reflex camera— or an *SLR*. It is the only type of camera we will use in this classroom." The teacher looked around the room. "Good. I see that many of you have one."

He pushed back his glasses and continued. "We are going to learn about photography my way. That means real film and real hands-on techniques," Mr. Williams said. He began naming the parts of the camera.

Beth looked down at the small silver camera sitting on her desk. "Well, that's just great," she whispered to Riley. "My grandmother gave this to me. It's not the kind we're supposed to use. I can't ask her to exchange it, though. What am I going to do now?"

"Don't worry about it," Riley whispered back. "I have an SLR camera. You can borrow it when I'm not using it, which should be most of the time. I don't think I'll need to spend too much time doing photography homework. How tough is it going to be to take some pictures? I mean, it's not like it's rocket science or anything," he said. Riley nodded toward Mr. Williams. The photography teacher was showing the class how to load film into the camera. "Do you see what I mean?" Riley said.

When class was finished, Riley waited for Beth to pack up her books. He shook his head in amazement. "Wow. At least the grade is going to be a piece of cake," Riley said.

"Shhhh!" Beth warned. She tilted her head toward the teacher. "I wouldn't be so sure. Mr. Williams is supposed to be pretty tough."

"Yeah, right. Did you look at the list of assignments he gave out?" Riley asked. He sorted through the class handouts. He read from the list of the photographs that the students were supposed to take. "He wants us to take a picture of a letter of the alphabet! Is he serious? *A letter of the alphabet!*" Riley said.

"Not an actual 'letter,' Riley. We're supposed to take a picture of something that *looks* like one. You know…like taking a picture of a wreath for the letter 'O,'" Beth said.

Riley still did not look convinced.

Beth changed her approach. "Normally you like a challenge."

"Are you saying that this class is supposed to be a *challenge?*"

"Of course it is! Think about all the adventure…" she trailed off.

"Adventure? Go on. I'm listening," he said.

"Take the news, for instance. Haven't you ever thought about who took those pictures? Do you remember when that volcano blew up last year? The pictures were in all the newspapers. Somebody had to escape the lava flow to get those shots, right? Or how about all those war pictures? Just who do you think dodged the bullets to take them? *People* took them, Riley. Face it, Riley. Photography is a risky business. Mr. Williams may just be the key to a life of adventure for you!" she teased.

"I doubt it. Besides, all I want to do is get into a good school next year."

"Whatever you say. Let's just have a bit of fun for a change. It's our last year of high school, after all. Besides, it's been a long time since we've had a class together," Beth said. She winked at him before heading to her next class.

As Riley made his way to French class, he thought about what Beth had said. Photography may not be so bad after all—as long as he could get great marks.

chapter 5

ooh la la!

Large, glossy posters covered the painted cement brick walls of the French room. There was a large poster of the Eiffel Tower lit up at night. Next to it was a picture of Quebec City in winter. It had a gigantic snowman in a red hat with a huge grin on its face.

Madame Gaudette sat at the front of the room. Her long, blond hair was pulled back into a low knot on her neck. Riley thought she was one of the best teachers at Bayview High. She was tough but fair. Riley liked the fact that she actually *listened* to what they had to say. Madame Gaudette always treated her students with respect. It was hard not to like her.

His mind wandered as he waited for class to begin. He thought about something that Beth had once said. She had told him that Madame Gaudette wore the best-looking shoes. Riley bent to the side and tried to see her feet. The teacher had on some sort of black strappy shoes. He shrugged. What was all the fuss about footwear? His mother had a ton of shoes. In fact, so did his father. Riley was content with his own white sneakers.

At the sound of the bell, the young teacher stood up. She welcomed everyone in French. *"Bonjour, classe!"*

"Bonjour, Madame Gaudette," the students answered together.

"Today we will discuss your assignments for the course," she said. Madame Gaudette passed them out to the class.

Riley checked it over. There was the course essay. It would count for fifty percent of his final mark. Each student had to write a thousand-word essay. It had to be written in French and be based on an actual French novel. Madame Gaudette also wanted them to turn in a two-page paper on the author.

Riley groaned. He did get top grades in French class, but he had to study hard to get them. Languages did not always make much sense to him. At least he could choose the book, though. He thought about reading *The Three*

Musketeers. He hoped that there would be lots about castles and sword fights. At least it would be enjoyable then.

On the corner of Lulu Fontaine's desk was a large book. A red ribbon was dangling out. Lulu was already at the halfway point of her novel.

Agh! The year just started, and she is ahead of me already! he thought. He spent the rest of the class figuring out how to make up for lost time.

Just before the bell rang, Madame Gaudette stood at the front of the room. "I have some exciting news," she said happily. "I return to France each summer to see my family. I also work in Paris as a tour guide at one of the art galleries. Perhaps you have heard of *Le Louvre?*"

Lulu nodded and quickly raised her hand.

"*Oui,* Lulu?" Madame Gaudette asked her. "Yes. Do you have a question?"

"Isn't the painting of the Mona Lisa kept at *Le Louvre?*" Lulu said.

Madame Gaudette said, "*Bien sûr!* You're right, Lulu! The painting of the Mona Lisa is there. Now I am happy to offer one of you the chance to see it in person. You will be spending two weeks this summer…in *Paris, France!*"

Everyone seemed to gasp at the same time. Madame Gaudette took another minute to quiet the students.

Darcy Maclean raised his hand. "That sounds great and everything, but who can afford to go? I mean, it must cost hundreds of dollars just for the plane ticket." The rest of the class nodded in agreement.

Madame Gaudette held up her hands. "I understand your concerns," she said. "That is why I met with members of the local French club. They want to help you learn more about the French way of life. The French club is going to be your sponsor! The top student of this class will win a flight to Paris. He or she will also receive spending money! And it gets even better," she said. Madame Gaudette beamed at the class as she paused. "The top student will also win an award. There will be money to go toward your school expenses for next year!"

Riley smiled to himself. *A summer in Paris, France! Now that would look terrific on my university forms. I have to win this contest.* He looked over at Lulu Fontaine. Riley was sure she was thinking the exact same thing.

chapter 6

can you say cheese?

After a week of classes, Riley and Beth were ready for their first photo shoot. They stood out under the huge, gnarled oak trees in the schoolyard. Beth made Tyson and Riley stand back to back. She posed them with their arms crossed. They were grinning like fools.

"That's it, guys! You're beautiful! Smile for the camera! Smile!" Beth said as she snapped photos. She giggled as the guys posed like models in a catalog.

"I *cannot* believe I agreed to do this," Tyson said. "I hope you aren't making me look like a fool. I have my reputation to keep up. You know…with the *ladies*."

Beth laughed. "Tyson," she said, "you look great! Just hold that pose…just another few seconds. Besides, the ladies will love you once they see your picture."

"You mean the ladies will love me even *more*," Tyson corrected her. "The ladies already love me." He ran his hands over his short, black dreadlocks. A wicked grin crossed his face.

"Uh huh. That's why you are spending all your free time with us. Right, buddy?" Riley said. "Maybe I can give you some pointers after I come back from Paris."

Tyson stopped posing. "Who is going to Paris?" he asked.

"I am!" Riley said proudly.

Beth shook her head. "I wouldn't be so sure about that, Riley. I heard Lulu talking about the trip the other day by our lockers. It sounds like she already has her bags packed. Hey, she has just as good a chance at going as you do. After all, you two have been the top students ever since grade nine. I even heard her say that she plans to study at the *Sorbonne*," Beth said.

"Who would want to study at the 'sore-buns'?" Riley said.

Tyson rolled his eyes. Then a smile crept onto his face. Soon he and Riley were doubled over with laughter.

"Ah, you really are the king," Tyson said. He was wiping tears from his eyes.

"That's right, I'm Joe King!" Riley said. He and Tyson broke out in laughter all over again. "Get it? I'm *'joe-king'*! I'm *joking*!" he said between breaths of laughter.

"Ugh!" Beth groaned at the really bad humor. "I can't believe that you twits are about to graduate." Beth sighed and explained. "It's not the 'sore-buns.' It's the *Sorbonne*. You know—the famous university in Paris."

Tyson finally calmed down. "I bet that winning this competition would help Lulu's chances of going to school there. I bet she'll be extra competitive now. We all know how much she likes a challenge," he said.

"May the best student win," said Beth.

"How can you be on her side, Beth?" Riley said. "You're supposed to be my friend."

"I am, you dope. I just think that you should back off when it comes to Lulu. She has her own problems to deal with. It's pretty impressive that she is at the top of the class. She is more than a year younger than we are, after all," Beth reminded him. Lulu had been bumped up a year in grade school because she was so smart.

"What's Lulu's problem? She doesn't have my parents to deal with," Riley said.

"No, not *your* parents..." Beth trailed off. "Well, I think I'm done," she said. Beth checked over the assignment list. "Let's see. I've taken a picture of a group of people. I think that's everything I need. Here, Riley. You can take your pictures now." Beth handed him his camera. "I think you'll have to adjust the camera settings. It's grown a bit darker outside since I started. You may have to let more light in through the camera lens. You don't want your pictures to be too dark," reminded Beth.

"Oh, right," said Riley. He began to fumble with the camera. He spent the next few minutes trying to focus it. "This isn't working," he told them. "Give me a few minutes to figure out what to do." It had seemed so easy when Mr. Williams showed the class how to use the camera. Riley had barely paid attention.

Beth started to tell Tyson where Lulu planned to travel in France. Meanwhile, Riley was now ready to shoot. He began to take pictures of them talking. Tyson noticed Riley, and he began posing again. Something about it did not seem right. Tyson just looked like a guy smiling for the camera. He no longer seemed like *Tyson*.

Riley shook his head. "No, no, no. Pretend that I'm not here," he said.

Tyson shrugged and turned back to Beth. He began telling her about some old jazz musician who had once played in France. Beth laughed at his crazy description of how the musician played. Tyson even added trumpet sounds, which made her laugh even more.

Riley took more pictures of them talking. The more they talked, the better things looked to Riley behind the camera lens. Beth and Tyson just seemed more real. Riley realized that he was not just taking a picture of his friends. He was taking a picture of their *friendship*.

Then Riley wondered how the pictures would be if he changed his position. He began to circle around them. Some shots were close up. Others were taken while Riley crouched low.

By the time he finished his roll of film, Riley was excited. He had never really thought about how he took pictures before. He figured that all you had to do was point the camera and press the button. No one had told him that there was a personal side to taking pictures. He had no idea that he could control what things would look like. Now there seemed to be so much more he could do with a camera.

Riley finished at last. The three friends piled into Tyson's small, midnight-blue car. Six-foot tall Tyson got in last. He had to fold up his legs to fit into the tiny front seat. Somehow, only Tyson could look cool doing it.

In fact, they were all surprised when he bought the tiny car a year ago.

"It's a classic," Tyson said at the time.

"It's so small," Beth told him.

"It's compact," Tyson replied.

"It's a clown car," Riley added.

"*Whatever*," Tyson sighed.

On their way home, Beth chose the radio station. Dance music blared from the speakers.

"What do your parents think of your photography class, now?" Beth asked.

Riley shuddered. "Don't mention it. My dad is still mad. His right eye twitches any time I mention the class. My mom hasn't said much about it, though. It almost seems like she is avoiding the subject."

"What about you, Tyson? Any major dramas in your life these days?" Beth said.

"No. Just school. I've got a lot of science classes this year, but they shouldn't be a problem. But then again, I don't have anyone riding my back," he said. "My dad is just happy that I'm going to 'protect and serve' like him."

"So are you still going to apply for the police force?" Riley said.

"Maybe. I really want to investigate crime scenes and search for clues. It would be cool to be one of the brains behind the big police busts.

I plan on getting into a good program next year," Tyson said.

"You will be great at it! You were born to figure things out," Beth said.

"Thanks for the vote of support. What about you, Beth? Are you still going to be the best math teacher ever?" Tyson said.

Beth nodded. "Of course. I just hope that I can save enough money for university. I'll go nuts if I have to wait an extra year to go."

Riley listened to his friends discuss their plans. They were so sure about what they wanted to be. Up until now, Riley was focused, too. He was on track with his parents' plan.

Yet something seemed strange to him now. The plan did not feel right anymore. Taking pictures did.

chapter 7

in the dark

The dim red light of the darkroom gently shone on Riley as he worked. He gently rocked the shallow tray on the table in front of him. It was filled with liquid. A paper floated inside it. Riley was counting the seconds. "Thirty...thirty-one...thirty-two..." An image began to appear on the paper. He began to see the outline of Beth's face looking straight at him. The longer the paper soaked, the more Riley could see of the picture. Beth's long, dark hair was blowing across her face. She was laughing as she tried to brush it away from her eyes.

Riley grabbed a pair of tongs and took the photo out of the tray. He gently placed the picture into a second one. This tray of chemicals was called a stop bath. A short soak in it would keep the picture from developing even more. Riley did not want his print to turn black. He counted to thirty and then took out Beth's picture. Riley dunked her image into the last tray. Now he was ready to rinse off any chemicals left on his print. He soaked it in a sink full of cold water until the print was finished.

There! It's done! Riley thought proudly.

The red light that dimly lit the room made it seem almost eerie. Students were extra quiet and careful when they were working on their prints. Just one splash of the wrong chemical on their paper would wreck the whole picture. No one wanted to have to make their print again.

Riley gathered his supplies and took the print that he just developed. He made his way to the darkroom door.

Mr. Williams had many rules for students in the darkroom. The biggest was to make sure that the darkroom stayed dark. No white light was allowed to shine in from the classroom, so there were two doors. One door was for entering the darkroom. The other was to get into the classroom. In between the two doors was a little cubbyhole. Mr. Williams insisted that the students knock before they entered the small space. No one was allowed to open the two doors at the same time.

Riley knocked and stepped into the cubbyhole. A guy barged in from the classroom side without knocking. It was a shaggy-haired student named Morgan. Riley did not have the darkroom door closed yet. A blinding flash of light flooded the darkroom.

"HEY! CLOSE THE OUTSIDE DOOR!" someone yelled.

"AGH! MY DOUGHNUT!" a tall blonde shouted at him.

"Oops! Sorry," Morgan said. "Your doughnut?" he asked. "Hey! You aren't supposed to eat in the darkroom...but do you have any more?"

"No, it's not a real doughnut. It's my photo of the letter 'O,'" the girl replied.

Morgan shook his head in disappointment and sighed. The darkroom filled with laughter.

Riley quickly slipped into the classroom. He squinted in the bright light.

"Well, Riley. How did this one turn out?" the photography teacher asked him. He pointed to the print in Riley's hand.

"I was hoping you would help me check it over," Riley said.

Mr. Williams followed him to his desk. Riley set down his wet picture. They looked it over and compared it to two similar prints he had just made. The first one had small white flecks in the middle of it. Mr. Williams had said that they were caused by dust on the negative. The second picture had a weird chemical splash mark in the corner.

"This last print looks like the best, Riley! It's crisp and clean," Mr. Williams said. "You have captured Beth's beauty. You really are a good photographer! You know how to make your models feel comfortable. Beth looks relaxed. You must be a natural!" Mr. Williams said.

"Yeah! I think it's good enough to hand in for one of my assignments," Riley said proudly. "This one will be for my portrait shot." He gave the print to Mr. Williams.

The photography teacher smiled at his student. "Good job!" he said.

Riley felt great. *Maybe Beth will want one of these other two*, he thought.

Growing up, Beth had always been "one of the guys." She always made the best snow forts. Riley had been knocked in the head more than once by her snowballs. She also had the best baseball cards. She was ruthless when it came to trading them. Riley had never considered what she looked like before.

As Riley studied the picture, he realized that Mr. Williams was right. Beth was—beautiful!

He thought back to when he had taken the picture. The three of them had been walking downtown after school. It had just stopped raining, and the sun was peeking out from the clouds. Shafts of light beamed down and shimmered on the puddles that had formed. The clouds broke enough for a rainbow to shine through. Riley took out his camera to capture it.

Beth and Tyson had stopped to look in the bookstore window while they waited for him. Just then, a stream of water poured off the awning. Riley caught the look of surprise on Tyson's face when it dumped right on his head. Tyson was stunned. Water matted down his perfect hair. His jean jacket was soaked. Beth began to giggle at Tyson, who always seemed so cool. Her giggling turned into a great big belly laugh. A gust of wind blew her hair softly across her face. That's when Riley snapped her picture. He could still almost hear her laughter.

Suddenly, Riley felt strange staring at Beth's picture. He tucked the pictures into his photography portfolio and left.

chapter 8

out of the dark

By the middle of October, Riley had spent most of his free time taking pictures. His portfolio was getting thick with his photographs. He was becoming a regular in the darkroom, too. He even made a deal with Mr. Williams to get more time to develop pictures. Riley could use the darkroom after school with the camera club. He just had to help Mr. Williams clean up afterward.

Other classes did not seem as interesting anymore. He had already missed a chemistry lab report and had not picked a topic for his history term paper. His copy of *The Three Musketeers* for French class still lay at the bottom of his backpack—barely opened. The only class that he put any real effort into was photography.

Riley and Tyson made their way to the back of Lee's Restaurant after school. Riley dropped his books on their usual booth. His photography portfolio slid off the top of the pile.

Tyson picked it up and began flipping through it. "Man, what a great picture! Can I get a copy of this?" he asked.

"Of Beth? Sure. I have an extra copy for her, too," Riley said without thinking.

"No, of this one!" Tyson said. He was holding up a picture of himself. Tyson was in sunglasses and leaning against his car. "This is a great picture of the 'love mobile.'"

Riley had handed it in for an assignment. Tyson had insisted that Riley use the blue car. Riley agreed. He knew that the car was Tyson's pride and joy. They decided to shoot it in front of one of the historic houses in town. Their own houses were too new for Tyson's car.

Tyson had driven through the old section of town. He stopped in front of a tall, two-storey red brick house covered in green ivy. A black iron railing ran around the front porch. Gaslights with their small flickering blue flames lit up the front door.

Tyson was about to hand the photo back to Riley when he stopped. "Wait a minute. Who is that guy near the bushes?

"What are you talking about?" Riley asked.

"It looks like there's a guy in the background. See? Near the bushes over there," Tyson said. He pointed to some tall bushes growing around the sides of the house. "I'm not sure, but it looks like he might be hiding."

Riley grabbed the picture and squinted. There did seem to be someone near the side window. He was dressed in dark clothing. "Oh, yeah. But I don't think he's hiding, Tyson. It looks like he's crouching to tie his shoe."

Tyson turned into a detective. A ton of questions began to fly out of his mouth. "Who could he be? Why is he there? Is he checking out Willow's house? I wonder if he is planning to rob it," he said.

"Wait a minute. It's just a guy by some bushes. And why would you mention *Willow*?" Riley jumped in.

"Because that's Willow Thomson's house! I thought you knew where the prettiest girl at Bayview lives," Tyson said. He seemed annoyed that Riley had interrupted him.

"So that's why you insisted we stop at *that* house. I think that you're reading too much into this. If you are that concerned, then maybe you should tell Willow about it. Maybe she knows who he is and why he's there," Riley said.

Tyson thought about it. "I probably should. Then again…what if she doesn't know the guy? It could freak her out. Maybe we should find out who it is first," he said.

We? Riley could tell that a plan was beginning to form in Tyson's head. He had been through enough of his "plans" over the years. He winced at what Tyson was about to suggest.

"This calls for a stakeout!" Tyson said.

"Are you for real? Who holds a stakeout? You have to be part of some cheesy late-night movie to do that," Riley laughed.

"Riley, it's our duty to be there. This guy may be planning to rob Willow's house. We need to find out. Willow could be in real danger," Tyson said.

"Do you really expect me to sit around in the dark? This guy could just be walking by her place for all we know. Even if he does show up, what are we supposed to do? Bring squirt guns and make a citizen's arrest? No way. You should tell your dad if you really think Willow is in danger. Let the police do their job," said Riley.

"Listen. I know it sounds a bit crazy. I just want to be able to give some hard evidence to the police. What kind of detective will I be if other people do the work for me?" Tyson said. "Look. If he does show up again, I promise not to do anything stupid. I'll stay in the car and call the police. Okay?"

Riley could not put his finger on it, but Tyson's story did not add up. "Why are you so eager to help Willow Thomson all of a sudden? When did she ever do anything for you? In fact, when did she ever *say* anything to you?" He began to fit all the pieces together. "Wait a minute…you like Willow!" Riley said.

Tyson looked a bit embarrassed. "No, I don't! I hadn't even noticed her long, soft hair and those dark, gorgeous eyes. No. You're way off on this one. I just want to improve my crime-solving skills," he said.

"I knew it!" Riley said happily. "You like her! You *love* Willow!"

Tyson shrugged his shoulders. "Will you help me?" he asked quietly.

Riley studied his friend. There was something more to all of this. Tyson never had to go out of his way to get a girl's attention. Girls were always hanging around him or calling him up. Now Tyson was going out of his way for Willow. In fact, Tyson was acting like a fool in love just over the *idea* of helping her.

Maybe sitting out in a car for one night would be very interesting, he thought. "Okay," Riley agreed. "We're on."

chapter 9

stink bomb

Riley had taken on his own personal project, too. He was going to master nighttime shots. Mr. Williams had given him a roll of film that he could use in the dark. Riley had been up late the last few nights trying to take pictures of the moon. Most of them did not turn out the way he had hoped. They were usually blurry or too dark. He was determined to get it right.

Late nights with the camera meant less time for other homework. Riley never did seem to find the time to study for his history test. Luckily, his parents had been working long hours on their new case. It was just as well. He felt strange talking to them about school these days. Term papers were due in a few weeks, and report cards were around the corner. Riley knew his parents would be in his face one of these days. He was hoping to put off the meeting as long as possible.

Riley was thankful that Mr. Williams let him spend a lot of time in the darkroom. It seemed to be his own personal hangout these days.

The November full moon was going to take place soon. Riley wanted to talk to Mr. Williams about how to photograph it. Riley found him in the supply cupboard.

"Hello, Riley. You're just the person I was hoping to see. I have an exciting offer for you! Last night, my wife had a look at your work while I was marking assignments. She thinks that you have a good eye for the camera. In fact, she wants to offer you a job!"

"Your wife wants to offer me a job? Doing what? What does she do?" Riley asked.

Mr. Williams smiled. "My wife is Victoria Williams. She is a photographer. Do you know her work?"

Riley was stunned. Of course he knew about Victoria Williams! Her photos were in all the magazines. He just had no idea she was *that* Victoria Williams!

"Wait a minute! You didn't show her 'Stink Bomb' did you?" Riley said in horror. That was the picture he handed in for his 'piece of nature' photo. It was a picture of steam rising off a pile of Stinky's daily dirt.

Mr. Williams sighed and nodded. "That was not your most tasteful assignment. Luckily she also saw your photo of Beth. She thinks that you have some real talent as a photographer. That's why she asked about you. Victoria is in a jam right now and needs some extra help. Would you like the job?"

"Are you kidding? Of course I would! When do I start?" Riley said.

"Great! I'll tell Victoria. Her next photo shoot is this Sunday morning. It's at the old Riverside Estate. I think it's for a perfume ad for a fashion magazine. I must warn you. Victoria starts working early. You should be there by seven o'clock sharp."

"Did you say 'Sunday?'" Riley asked.

"Yes. The homeowners are only out of town on Sundays. It's the only free day," he answered.

Riley grinned all through French class. *I can't believe it. A real photographer thinks my pictures are good!* he thought.

In fact, his daily French mini-test was a blur. He forgot all about last week's test that Madame Gaudette was about to hand back. This was the third one that Riley had not studied for this term. He was not really worried about his mark, though. He still believed that he could pull it all together before report cards.

There were only ten minutes left before the end of class. Madame Gaudette picked up the neat stack of test papers on the corner of her desk. She handed them back the way she always did. They were in order of the highest mark to the lowest. Riley did not really like when she did that. It did not really bother him, though. He always had a top mark.

Lulu received her paper first. She turned around and smiled smugly at Riley.

No problem. I didn't think I'd be on top this week, anyhow, he thought. *Next week I'll just have to get an A+. That should even out my grade average,* he figured.

Then she handed a paper to another girl. She continued handing out papers to the rest of the class. For the first time ever, Riley received his paper last.

Riley turned over the page and was stunned. There was no "A" in the top corner. Madame Gaudette had written a big red "D."

"You have got to be kidding! There must be a mistake here," Riley cried.

Madame Gaudette turned around and stared at him. "*Non,* Riley. I'm afraid that I gave you the correct mark. The answers are either right or wrong. I suggest that next time you study," she said.

"But I did!" Riley lied. *Why did I say that?* he wondered to himself.

"Really?" Madame Gaudette said with surprise. "If you need extra help you know where to find me. I'm sure that I don't need to remind you that report cards are coming." She returned to the front of the room.

Just over an hour ago, Riley had been on top of the world. Now he had a poor grade and had just lied to his teacher. He felt like throwing up. Riley finally knew what it felt like to be at the bottom. He did not like it one bit.

chapter 10

I should have
taken Italian

After the bell rang, Lulu came over and leaned on Riley's desk. Riley knew she could not resist rubbing in the fact that *she* was number one.

"What do *you* want, Lulu?" he said. She was the last person he wanted to see.

"I'm sorry about your French test, Riley. I just wanted to know if you needed me to help you study," she teased.

"Right. In your dreams," he said.

"I just thought I'd help. By the way, how is your essay coming along? I'm almost done mine. Will you be ready to hand in yours on Monday?" she asked. The words came out almost sweetly. She had a twinkle in her eye.

"What? On Monday? No way. It's due next month," he said.

"Next month starts this coming Monday," Lulu said over her shoulder as she walked away.

Riley panicked. He quickly flipped through his notes until he found the details of the essay. *The report is actually due in four days! I have barely started the book,* he said to himself.

Riley skipped lunch and went straight to the library. He only had a copy of *The Three Musketeers*. He still needed some more books to write the paper on the author, too. Riley found a thick, dusty book on Alexandre Dumas. The spine was stiff and seemed to crack when he opened the front cover. The pages had that old, dusty smell of his grandparents' attic.

Darcy Maclean was also making his way through the same section of books. "Hello, Riley," he said. Darcy picked out another thick book by the same author.

"*The Count of Monte Cristo*?" Riley read. "Didn't they make that into a movie?" Riley asked him.

"Really? That's good to know. I don't think I'll have time to read the book at all," Darcy answered. He looked totally calm about it.

Riley was curious about Darcy's plan. *He's not really going to base his essay on a movie, is he?* Riley thought. "So how are you going to write your paper?" Riley asked him.

"With research," Darcy told him as he pulled a few more books. "I'm going online for most of my stuff. You know...on homework websites," he said.

"That's a bold move, my man," Riley said. *And stupid,* he added in his head.

"I don't think so. I thought I'd check out some of those term-paper sites for a few pointers," Darcy added.

"As long as you don't try to buy one," Riley said with concern.

Darcy shrugged. "Hey, I'm just trying to get my homework done. There doesn't seem to be any extra time these days. I've got my band, my job, and my other classes. I may have to be a bit creative about how I write this paper," he said. "Besides, it's just a French paper."

"Good luck," Riley said under his breath. "You're going to need it."

chapter 11

musketeers to
the rescue

The night—Saturday. The time—ten o'clock. The place—Chestnut Lane. The dark blue car quietly turned onto Willow's street. Tyson turned off the lights. He cut the engine a few houses away from hers. The small car coasted to a stop just before the streetlight. The two boys were hidden by the dark night.

Riley's side of the car was crammed full of "stakeout supplies." There was a large bag of food and a thermos of hot chocolate. His own backpack was somewhere in the backseat.

"How long do you think we'll have to stay here? I don't think I can sit like this for too long," Riley said. His knees were bent up to his chest. *Stupid clown car,* he added in his head.

"As long as it takes," Tyson answered.

"Well, maybe I'll have a snack. Do you want something?" Riley said. He opened the food bag and pulled out a sandwich and a bottle of water.

"No, thanks," Tyson said. "I need to concentrate on this scene. Pass me my undercover kit, please." Riley handed him a black leather bag. Tyson pulled out the contents and set them on the dashboard of the car. He laid out a flashlight and a pair of binoculars. Next came a cell phone and some walkie-talkies.

Riley was impressed. "When did you get all this stuff?" he asked. "I didn't know you were this serious about the detective thing," Riley said. He reached for the binoculars, but Tyson grabbed his hand.

"I'm very serious when it comes to solving crimes. Don't mess with my equipment," Tyson said. He put the strap over his head and looked through the binoculars.

"What should I do?" Riley said.

"You can take notes," Tyson told him.

"Take notes of what?" he asked.

"License plates. The weather. The cars on the street. Write down all those details that most people overlook. It's the little pieces of information that help solve the crime, Riley. Remember that I said that. In fact, write it down so you don't forget."

"*Riiight*," Riley said. He leaned back in his seat instead. "I think I'll just watch."

"Good idea. You're too much of a beginner to help out much. Just keep your eyes open for anything strange," Tyson said.

Riley enjoyed the silence—for a while. He soon got bored. Riley wondered if Tyson needed a break, too. "Mr. Williams' wife saw some of my photographs. She offered me a job as her assistant. I start tomorrow."

"Cool!" Tyson said.

"Yeah, but now I'm not so sure. My parents are still peeved that I'm in the photography class. They would really be upset if it was my job, too. Besides, they don't even want me to have a job while I'm in school. You know the Jackson family saying," Riley said.

He and Tyson spoke at the same time. "Focus on your future. The rest comes next."

Tyson laughed. "How could I forget! Well, you know what my mom always says, right? 'Live the moment.'"

Tyson turned back to Willow's house. They sat in silence again. The stakeout was just as Riley figured it would be. Nothing strange took place. In fact, the most suspicious thing on the street was them.

chapter 12

fearless?

A thin string of drool dribbled out of the corner of Riley's mouth. His head bobbed and then jerked back. He woke up startled. He was confused for a moment. Then he remembered where he was. He looked over at Tyson. His friend was still staring through the binoculars.

"Tyson, what did I miss?" Riley whispered.

Tyson said nothing.

"Oh, I get it. I'll wait until you're done," Riley said. "Okay, Tyson? Tyson? TYSON!" Riley said.

"Huh?" Tyson jumped in his seat. The binoculars flew out of his hands. They swung around his neck and smashed against the back of his head. "OUCH!" Tyson yelled and grabbed his skull. "What the—!" he cried. He looked around and realized what had happened. He decided to play it cool. "Is there any more hot chocolate?" Tyson asked. He yawned and stretched out his long arms.

"No, we finished it earlier. By the way, you sound like you are sawing logs when you sleep," Riley said.

"I do not!" Tyson said. "I *may* have been breathing loudly."

Riley looked back at Willow's house. "Uh, Tyson...did you see that? The bushes under the side window moved."

"Are you serious?" he said. Tyson reached back for the binoculars that were now hanging down his back. He leaned back and focused on the tall red-brick house across the street.

"Look! There, it happened again!" Riley said. He couldn't believe what was happening.

"Where?" Tyson quickly scanned the house. He looked to the rooftop and back down to the cellar windows. He looked left and then right. "I don't see anything. Are you sure you saw something?" he said.

Slowly, a head appeared out of the bushes. Next came shoulders and a body. The guy must have thought the coast was clear. He reached up and grabbed onto the white trellis on the side of the house. He was about to climb up.

"Oh, man!" Tyson said. "There really is someone trying to get into Willow's house! Quick, Riley, let's go!"

"Do you actually mean that *we* are going to catch this guy?" Riley saw the look of determination on Tyson's face. "Oh, all right! You owe me big, Tyson," Riley said.

"Stay low and out of sight," Tyson told him. He was already out of the car.

"Thanks for the great advice," Riley muttered. He grabbed his camera from his backpack. Riley quietly opened the door and slid out. He and Tyson crouched beside the car. They crawled up the sidewalk and hid behind the car parked in front of them. Riley looked left. Tyson looked right. Then Tyson bolted across the street. Riley was right behind him.

By this time, the guy was halfway to the second floor.

Riley looked up at him and snapped a few pictures. Tyson was ready to climb up after the guy when a car turned onto the street. Riley and Tyson dove into the bushes as the headlights lit up the Thomson house. They breathed a sigh of relief when the car turned into the neighbor's driveway. They did not relax for long. A heavy, older man got out and walked toward the Thomson house.

"Who is there?" the neighbor called.

The guy climbing up the house froze. Lights began to turn on in the Thomson house. The stranger on the trellis scrambled down. He brushed by them and ran down the street.

Riley and Tyson were frozen, too. The neighbor was coming closer.

Then Tyson whispered to Riley, "Come on!"

They ran back to his parked car. Tyson started the car as Riley jumped in. "Hurry!" Tyson said.

"Did you see the size of that guy? He was huge! He could have attacked us!" Riley said. He pulled the door shut with a thud.

"Yeah, and there you were taking his picture," Tyson said.

"What? I figured it would help us find out who he was. I can develop them in class on Monday," said Riley.

Tyson shook his head in anger. "One more minute and I would have had him." With a rev of the engine, the daring duo sped off into the dead of night.

chapter 13

show time

"**H**owdy hi! This is the Bob Peters weekend radio show. What a great morn—" Riley gave one swift thud to the alarm clock. The blaring sound of Bob Peters shut off.

"*Ugh!*" Riley groaned. He opened one eye and squinted at the clock radio. Six o'clock. He threw his legs over the side of the bed and stumbled to the shower.

On his way downstairs, he hoped he could avoid facing his parents. He did not want to explain that he was going to work at a photo shoot. That bit of news would not go over well. Then the rich smell of freshly ground coffee filled his nose. *Oh, no. The parental units are up.* He took a deep breath and entered the kitchen. *Here we go.*

His father was sitting at the end of the sleek glass kitchen table. A steaming mug of coffee and a toasted bagel with cream cheese sat in front of him. He looked over the top of the weekend newspaper as Riley approached. "Well, well, well! Look who is up at the crack of dawn on a Sunday!" he said. "Where are you going so early?" his father asked. He sipped his strong, black coffee.

"Oh…uh…the library…research…essays, you know," Riley lied.

"Really? At this time of day? On a Sunday?"

Riley gulped. "Oh…sure," Riley said. *Well, it's not a total lie if I go after the photo shoot,* he thought. Riley grabbed his jacket and hurried for the back door.

"That's my boy! Keep up those grades," Mr. Jackson said. He resumed reading the paper. Riley was almost out the door. He could feel the crisp morning air on his face when his father's voice stopped him. "Aren't you forgetting something?"

"Wha…what's that?" Riley said. His voice was filled with alarm.

"Your books."

"Oh! Right!" Riley said. He reached into the kitchen and grabbed his backpack. He bolted for his car before his father could speak again.

69

It took Riley half an hour to get to the old Riverside Estate. He turned off the main road and drove toward the mansion. The wheels of his silver car crunched on the stones of the circular driveway. The white mansion seemed big from the road, but up close it was huge.

Riley pulled in beside a row of expensive cars parked in front. He was about to step out when a shiny red car roared in beside him. The driver flashed her white teeth at Riley in a playful smile. Her long, blond hair was pulled back in two loose braids. Her friend gave Riley a wink before they both went into the house.

Wow! Talk about a dream job! he smiled to himself. *I can't believe I'm here.*

As he got out of his own car, Riley noticed a petite, dark-haired woman. She was lifting large metal suitcases out of the back of a truck. Riley hurried over to help.

"Let me give you a hand," he offered. Riley took the large metal case, which he nearly dropped on the ground. *What has she got in here—bowling balls?* he thought.

"Thank you! You must be Riley. I'm Victoria. I'm so glad to meet you!" she said with a warm smile. With that she held out her hand.

Her handshake was much firmer than he would have thought from such a tiny woman.

She was nothing like he imagined. He was expecting someone more like her husband. Victoria was very different. She had on a black cap with a funky, colorful design around the brim. Her long, black skirt covered her black boots. *Now she looks like an artist,* Riley thought.

"Are you ready to work?" she asked him.

"Of course!" Riley answered. "Mr. Williams said that we are going to be shooting a perfume ad today. Is that right?"

Victoria nodded. "Yes. It's a new perfume called 'First Love.'" Then she turned and lifted another suitcase out of her truck. Riley grunted as he picked it up and followed her into the white house.

"Take this camera equipment up to the second floor," she told him. "My assistant will tell you what to do with it. I'm going to have a word with the caretaker." She turned down a long hallway to the right.

Riley lugged the cases up a spiral staircase. The morning light shone through the floor-to-ceiling windows at the top. He shaded his eyes and went through the double glass doors to the deck outside.

"Wow!" Riley said. The deck overlooked the winding Grand River. Over time, the broad river had carved a deep trench through the landscape. The tree-covered riverbanks were as high as cliffs. Sea gulls flew below. Riley had driven along the river hundreds of times. It had never looked as impressive as it did from this height. He could not take his eyes off the scene.

His view of the river was interrupted by a female voice. "You can bring that equipment over here," she said.

chapter 14

not just a pretty face

There she was again—Willow Thomson. Riley felt a wave of red sweep over him. It traveled up his neck, across his face, and out to the tips of his ears. Riley opened his mouth to speak, but only a string of garbled noises spilled out. Being an "A"-student had not prepared him for surprise meetings with models. His last meeting with Willow had not been a good one, either.

"What are *you* doing here?" Willow said. Her hands were on her hips.

"I'm...uh...working?" he said, like it was a question. As far as he knew, Willow did not know about the stakeout. Riley wanted to keep it that way.

Willow was doubtful. "Really? Well, we *are* supposed to have a new assistant today."

"That's right!" Riley said. He did not know what to say next. "Hey. Aren't you supposed to be with the other models?" he asked.

Now Willow smiled. "I haven't modeled in almost a year. I'm Victoria's main assistant, now," she said proudly.

"Really?" he said with surprise. Then Riley realized what she meant. "Oh, great. That means I'm *your* assistant." He was not sure that working for Willow was a good thing.

"Don't worry," Willow said, softening a bit. "I'm happiest when I'm behind the camera."

"Really? Why would you give up the modeling? I thought every girl dreamed of being a model," Riley said.

"Who told you that fairy tale?" Willow said. "Don't get me wrong. Modeling has been a good thing for me, and I still do it sometimes. I like being able to travel. I've met a lot of interesting people, too. I just don't want to make a career out of it anymore. For one thing, I don't like having to get up at dawn. Working under hot lights all day is terrible. Modeling isn't as glamorous as it sounds," she said.

"I hadn't thought about it that way," he said.

"You will after today," Willow said.

Riley grinned. "So what do you want me to do first, Boss?"

"You can start by unpacking these cases," Willow told him. "I'll be back in a minute." She left him to go downstairs.

Riley was unpacking the metal suitcases when he heard voices. They seemed to be coming from a room off the deck.

GIRLS! Riley grinned to himself. *This is going to be great! A real photo shoot and gorgeous models! Can it get any better than this?*

He followed the voices and poked his head through one of the open double doors. There was one of the largest and most glamorous bedrooms he had ever seen. The entire room was covered in thick, white carpeting. There was a king-sized bed, too. Riley was tempted to fall asleep on the pile of overstuffed pillows. He was not used to getting up so early.

More importantly, the room was filled with young women. Riley guessed they must have been the models, but some of them looked terrible! He could not believe his eyes.

The blonde he saw outside now had rollers in her hair. A model with short, spiky red hair looked pale without any makeup. They all seemed to be going through some major beauty operation. A makeup artist was applying some sort of cream to one model's face. Another model was sitting in a chair. Her head was being yanked around as a stylist pulled, teased, and sprayed her hair.

So much for natural beauty, Riley thought.

Then an older woman with gray hair hustled in from the hallway. She pushed her way through the models to the large metal clothing racks in the far corner. They were crammed full of clothes. The hangers screeched across the metal bar as the woman whipped through the outfits. She had a bunch of pins sticking out of her mouth. She picked out a green velvet dress and slung a long black dress over her shoulder.

A short, curly-haired model noticed him and scowled. "What do you think you're looking at?" she said.

"Sorry!" Riley said quickly. He backed out of the room with embarrassment. *Wow, beautiful and friendly,* he thought.

Riley went back to find Willow. He found her setting up some very large umbrellas at one end of the deck.

"Are those props for the photo shoot?" Riley asked her.

"No. Those are for lighting. They will help reflect light where Victoria needs it for the pictures. Models don't look good with shadows on their faces. It might make them look less than 'perfect.'" Willow grinned. "Why don't you grab Victoria's tripod and set up over here?"

Riley found the camera stand. "I'll do my best," he said and smiled nervously.

It took forever, but at last they were finished getting ready. Riley was exhausted. Willow leaned on the railing next to him and sipped a bottle of water. She did not look tired one bit.

In a moment, Victoria came out of the bedroom. The models followed behind her. Riley was speechless. The same women he had last seen in curlers now looked gorgeous.

"It's show time!" Willow said.

chapter 15

lights, camera, action

Victoria took roll after roll of film. The models held strange poses. They stood that way for painfully long periods of time. A few of the girls complained of being tired. The stylists often rushed in to touch up the models' clothing, hair, and makeup. It was unbelievable how much work it took. All of this was for some perfume Riley had never heard of before.

Willow was a true professional. She always seemed to know what camera or lens was needed next. Victoria even took some of Willow's suggestions. It was a real advantage that Willow was a model. She knew what worked for the models and what did not.

Riley worked much harder than he ever expected. He helped move the lighting, and he gathered props. At the end of the day he collapsed. Willow sat down beside him on an empty camera case.

Victoria came over. "Great job, you two! So what do you think, Riley? Will you be able to work with us again next weekend?" she asked.

"Really? I'd love it. I think I'll need more sleep next time, though. I'm beat!" Riley said with a moan.

"What did you expect? Pillow fights and girls jumping around in their bathing suits?" Willow said with a grin.

"Well, not exactly. I just didn't realize that it took so much work!" Riley said.

Victoria nodded. "Just think of all the times you flipped through magazines. I bet you never thought twice about the pictures. I'm sure you'll look at them a lot more carefully now," she said. "I took hundreds of pictures today. Only a handful of them will be good enough to be published. Even those ones will still be picked over and touched up."

"I don't get it. Why not just take a picture of how things *really* look?" he asked.

"You tell me," Victoria said, giving the question back to him. She smiled and left.

"That's a good question," Willow said thoughtfully. She turned to look at Riley. Willow did not look like she was annoyed by him anymore. "You know, Victoria was right. You really did a great job today. She made a good choice when she asked you to help," she said. "It's a real compliment coming from her."

"Thank you," he said and smiled back at her. He felt he could talk to her now. "I've been thinking a lot about taking pictures. I really like it, but I didn't think I could ever do it as a career. I don't know now. It's a lot more challenging than I realized. I like that. I can see now why you prefer to be behind the camera," he said.

"So what do you like to take pictures of?" she asked. "Maybe you can show them to me."

"That would be great!" Riley said. He thought of his photo of Beth. A warm feeling came over him. "I like to photograph people," he answered quietly.

Then he remembered all the photos he took at Willow's house. He felt bad keeping the picture of the guy hiding by her house a secret.

"Willow? There's something I have to tell you. Maybe it would be better if I showed you. I'll be right back."

"Sure," she said. Riley raced down the stairs to his car. When he returned, he pulled out a black book from his backpack. Riley handed her his portfolio.

"Oh! Your pictures!" she said. Willow looked carefully at each page. Riley waited for her to get to the photo from the stakeout. When she did, Willow gasped. "Hey! That's my house! When did you take this? *Why* did you take this?" Willow asked.

Riley was not sure what to say or where to begin. "There is a reasonable explanation…"

She folded her arms, tilted her head, and looked him straight in the eye. "Oh, this had better be good," she said.

Riley took a deep breath. He hoped Willow would not freak out on him—especially for Tyson's sake. Riley turned to the photograph of Tyson leaning against his car. "I took this picture for my photography class. I was supposed to hand in a picture of a type of transportation."

Willow looked closely at the picture. "Is that Tyson Richards?" she asked. Willow smiled.

Riley nodded. "Actually, Tyson was the one who noticed the guy in the picture. Look here." He pointed to the person hiding in the bushes. "Tyson thought you could really be in danger. In order to make sure, we…um…held a stakeout in front of your house."

"A *stakeout*?" she said with surprise.

Riley felt embarrassed. "I know it sounds weird. Listen, I'm sorry if we freaked you out.

Tyson was…I mean…*we* were worried that someone was after you."

"Let me see the picture again." She took the photo and squinted at the figure by the bushes. Then she looked at the photo of the guy on the trellis. Willow put down the picture and began to giggle.

What the heck is going on? Riley thought.

"That's Cody—my brother!" she said.

"This is your *brother?*" Riley said. He was stunned. After all he and Tyson had been through to help her. Now it turns out that this guy was just her *brother?* "Why doesn't he use the door like everybody else?" he asked.

"Cody is always getting home late. He sneaks in and out by climbing the trellis and using his window."

Riley smiled. "I can't wait to see the look on Tyson's face when I tell him!" he said.

After a moment, Willow grew quiet. "I can't believe you guys did this for me. Not many people at Bayview even bother to talk to me. But you sat outside in the dark because you thought I was in danger. Thank you."

"You really seem nice, Willow. I don't know why people don't like you. Maybe they would talk to you more if you were friendlier to them," he suggested.

"Is that what you think? That I'm not friendly enough?" Willow said. "People just don't get it at all. On some days I have to get up at five in the morning for my shoots. There is no way I could do my job if I stayed out as late as everyone else did. I can't think of the last time I stayed for an entire school dance. I feel like the girls at school think I'm a snob just because I model. *They're* the ones who don't talk to *me*. They're the real snobs!"

Riley thought about what she said. "Maybe there are some snobs out there, but there are also a lot of really great people, too. Like me! I also know somebody who doesn't think you're a snob. In fact, he was willing to face danger just to help you." Riley turned to the picture of Tyson and his car.

"Tyson?" she asked quietly.

Riley nodded.

chapter 16

a slippery slope

Guilt ate away at Riley when he got home from the photo shoot. First, he had lied to his parents about where he had been all day. They would freak out if they knew he was working. He still had to finish his French novel. He had not even started his essay. It was due in the morning. To top it off, his mother stopped by his bedroom to give a big support talk. She told him that she knew how hard he had been working lately. Riley was surprised to hear that she was really proud of him. If she only knew what he had really been doing.

Riley collapsed on his bed. Stinky jumped up beside him. "Hello, Stinkereeno. Are you going to keep me company tonight?" Riley said. The dog wagged her tail. "Good."

Then he reached into his backpack and pulled out *The Three Musketeers.* Stinky lay her head across Riley's legs and closed her eyes. He patted her head. "Get comfortable, buddy. It's going to be a *lonnnng* night."

Several hours later, Riley woke up. He was surprised to find himself fully dressed and still sitting on top of his bed. The red numbers on his clock radio glared four o'clock.

He picked up his French novel, which had slipped onto the floor. There still were one hundred and fifty pages left. It had taken him an hour just to read ten pages. At this rate, he would never be finished the book by Monday. He did not even want to think about having to write the essay in French! He had left his French-English dictionary at school, too. Riley looked at his computer. A light bulb went off in his head. *The Internet! Maybe I can find a dictionary online. There's hope, after all!*

Riley quickly found what he needed. He continued to search through the websites. He figured there would be some information on *The Three Musketeers,* too. He typed in his book title and hundreds of entries appeared.

He found some term-paper websites like the ones that Darcy Maclean had told him about. They were so easy. Riley just had to type in the topic of his essay. An essay on the same topic appeared in seconds. Some of the websites charged a "small" fee for using their papers. Then he remembered the students at Lincoln High. They were suspended for buying exams. *I certainly don't want to buy my homework,* he thought to himself.

Riley yawned. It was almost dawn, but he continued to search. At last he found some homework sites that looked honest. It just seemed to be students writing to other students. They were asking people for help on topics. *This looks promising. Maybe there are some references here that could help me out. It would just be sharing ideas, right? Kind of like a study group. It's just that these people are strangers.*

A queasy feeling began to grow in his stomach. It was telling him that something was not right.

On the other hand, maybe I'll just finish the book. I can figure it out myself, he decided. Riley picked up his French novel and tried reading it again. It was no use—it was going to take too long just to finish. There was no way he was going to make the deadline. Riley started to panic. There was no way he could hand his paper in late. He could not afford to receive a penalty on his grade. He had to beat Lulu for the

French competition. He had to get an "A." His parents would not allow anything else.

Riley turned back to the computer screen. After a bit more searching, he found another site. It claimed it had thirty thousand essays— free. *If it's free, then is it stealing if I take it?* he wondered. "Stinky, I think it's time to consider 'Plan B.'"

chapter 17

I hate Mondays

The school gym was packed on Monday morning. Riley slumped down in his chair and closed his eyes. *Ahh! This feels good,* he thought. The hum of students talking was the only thing keeping him awake. That and Beth nudging him in the ribs with her elbow.

"Riley! Wake up!" she whispered.

"Mmmmm…" he mumbled.

Tyson laughed and leaned back in his chair. "Hot study date last night?"

"Ha. Ha. I wish. Why are we here, anyhow? What is the subject of today's assembly? Are we going to hear about sweaty armpits?" Riley said.

Tyson was about to answer him but was cut off. A deafening squeal blared from the loudspeakers in the gym.

Riley grabbed his ears and moaned. "Why does everything seem louder when you have had no sleep?" He looked up at the principal on the stage. Principal Honsberger was trying to fix the microphone.

"Good morning," the principal bellowed. Another screech drowned out his voice. The audience giggled. Principal Honsberger took a deep breath, and his booming voice filled the gym. "Cheaters never prosper..." he said in a stern voice.

Riley looked at Tyson, and they both rolled their eyes. Even Beth gave an annoyed sigh.

"It's way too early for a lecture. This sounds like a corny one, too," Tyson said.

Riley nodded. Though, he was a bit curious about what Mr. Honsberger was going to say. The principal really looked peeved.

"We have a serious problem," Mr. Honsberger said. "Many of you may not even know that there is a problem. It involves all of you. It's plagiarism." The word rang in the air.

Some kids shook their head in confusion. It *sounded* important. Yet many people had no idea what he was talking about.

A redheaded girl with freckles held up her hand. "Is that when people copy homework?" she asked.

The principal frowned. "It is more than that. This is about taking other people's work and handing it in as your own. It may be just a few lines in an essay. In other cases it could be an entire term paper."

"Big deal," a student at the back shouted.

Principal Honsberger peered into the audience. "That's exactly why we are here today. It is a big deal," he boomed. "Plagiarism is the same as stealing. This time you are not taking things. You are taking ideas. Apparently many of you are doing it. Some of you may not be doing it on purpose. Perhaps some of you are making an honest mistake. Be aware that you must give credit to every idea that is not yours. Some of you have been handing in entire papers that you did not write at all."

Riley was wide awake now. He was shifting nervously in his seat. Beth leaned over and whispered for him to stop fidgeting.

The principal went on. "We have a code of conduct at Bayview High. It is clearly written in your student handbooks. We do not tolerate lying and cheating in this school. How you act within these school walls is a reflection of how you will act outside them. If you plagiarize a paper, you will receive a zero. That mark will go on your permanent record," he said.

Riley thought he felt the principal's eyes on him. He looked around quickly. *Is everyone looking at me?*

"You could face detention or be suspended. Cheating is a serious matter," Mr. Honsberger said to them.

As the students filed out of the gym, Beth shook her head. "Why was there such a big deal about cheating now? Did something happen here at Bayview?"

Tyson nodded. "There was some cheating here at Bayview. It happened in Miss Roth's English class. A couple of students handed in the same essay. They only changed the title."

"I bet it was part of that stuff at Lincoln High," Riley said.

"No. This is different. My brother Jamal heard that these guys bought their English papers off the Internet. Miss Roth searched on the Internet until she found the one they used. I also heard that some students in Mr. Cooper's history class were caught, too. Their papers weren't the same, but they were close. I heard that Mr. Cooper got a hunch about it. He even went to an Internet site for teachers and found some proof," Tyson told them.

"A teacher's site?" Riley said slowly. "What are you talking about?"

"Oh, yeah! I've heard of them," Beth said. "You know how there are websites where students can buy a term paper? Well, there are sites out there for teachers, too. They can check to see if a student's essay matches other essays out there. If there's a match, then the student may be guilty of cheating. Besides, teachers always seem to know when people cheat. It's like a sixth sense with them," she laughed.

Riley forced a smile. All he could think about was the French essay tucked in his backpack.

chapter 18

matchmaker,
matchmaker

Riley and Beth made it to the photography lab halfway through the class. Beth asked him casually, "How did your French essay turn out? Will it be another 'A+'-paper?"

Riley snapped at her. "It's none of your business. I really don't want to talk about it." He regretted saying it the moment the words came out of his mouth. He felt even worse when he saw Beth's eyes open in surprise. "Sorry, Beth. I just have a lot on my mind right now." He pretended to search for something in his backpack. He did not want to explain any more. Riley fumbled with some pictures. A few fell to the floor.

"*Mm hmmm,*" Beth replied. Clearly she was not buying it.

"I'm under a lot of pressure these days, you know," Riley continued. "Forget it. You wouldn't understand."

"Are you kidding me? Do you really believe that you are the only one around here with problems? Well, I've got some news for you, buddy. I've got essays, projects, and assignments up to here! It must be nice to be an 'A' student, Riley. I have to struggle just to get a 'B.' Besides, it's not as though I can afford to go to university! Maybe you shouldn't spend so much time with *supermodels*. You might notice how good you have it," Beth said. She stomped on his photos and stormed into the darkroom.

"Where did that come from?" he said and followed her in. "Beth?" he called. He found Beth working on a print. "Beth! I'm sorry for being such a jerk, but it's too difficult to explain," Riley said.

"You really are a piece of work, Riley," she whispered. "You really must see me as 'good old Beth.' You know, the friend who is good for pep talks. Let me tell you something, Riley. I'm more than 'just Beth'!" She turned back to her print.

Riley stared at her in disbelief. *What is she talking about?*

Beth looked up. "You can leave now," she told him.

"FINE!" Riley yelled and stormed out of the darkroom. A bright light filled the room, and the students inside groaned. "OH, GET OVER IT!" Riley yelled back at them and slammed the doors shut.

He grabbed his portfolio and turned to leave. A firm hand stopped him before he made it to the hallway. Riley turned to see Mr. Williams behind him.

"Are you and your girlfriend having a problem?" Mr. Williams said.

"What? Girlfriend? Who, Beth? She's not my girlfriend! Well, she is a girl...and she is my friend...but she's not my *girlfriend!* We're just *friends*, Mr. Williams. We are just friends."

Mr. Williams said nothing for a moment. Then he answered. "Of course you're 'just friends.' I *understand*." Mr. Williams winked at Riley. "I'd like to give you a little bit of advice on *friends*, Riley. Never let them walk away mad." Mr. Williams patted him on the back.

Girlfriend? Where did he come up with that? Riley thought to himself.

Riley did not know what to do. It was too early for French. He also was dreading handing in the essay. He stopped at his locker to get his jacket. "Some fresh air would feel good about now," he said under his breath.

He was on his way to the main doors when he ran into Beth near the French room.

"I think these are yours," she said. "Mr. Williams sent me to give these to you." She handed him his photos.

"Oh. Thanks," he said. He noticed Beth staring at him. She looked confused. "What is it now?" he asked her. Then Riley looked at the pictures. The top one was of Beth.

"I didn't know you had these," she said almost shyly.

"Yes. I…um…like how they turned out," Riley said. He looked into Beth's warm face. Her deep brown eyes were shining. A wave of warmth swept over him. "They look great." *You look great*, he added silently. "Listen, Beth, I'm really sorry for acting like such a jerk."

Beth nodded and smiled gently. Riley thought he saw her blush. "I'm sorry about before, too. You were right. I may have overreacted *a bit*. We've known each other a long time. Things have changed so much this year," she said and looked up at him. "You've changed, too. What's going on?"

"I'm not sure where to begin. This has all become so difficult. You may not believe this, but I'm really not an 'A' student. I mean…I *was* on top, but things just got out of control this term. I've missed a few assignments in some of my classes. I've been so busy with the photography class. I haven't been able to study as much as I should. To make a long story short, my grades have slipped—a lot." He looked around and then lowered his voice. "So, I've had to take some drastic measures."

"How bad could it be?" she asked.

"I went online…" Riley said slowly.

"Yes, and…" Beth said.

"I didn't want to do it…but I was going to miss the essay deadline. And if Lulu wins the Paris trip, I'll never live it down. Never mind what my parents will do to me. They'll freak when they find out," he blurted.

"Okay, so you did some research on the Internet. Maybe it wasn't the best place for information, but it could be worse. I wouldn't worry about it," Beth told him.

Riley shook his head. He paused before he told her the truth. "No, it's not what you think. I didn't write my French essay…someone else did. Beth, I downloaded an essay."

Beth's eyes grew wide. Her mouth dropped open in shock. "Are you NUTS?

Just then someone squeezed past them and went into the French room. It was Lulu.

"*Bonjour! Pardonnez-moi!*" Lulu said happily.

Riley groaned. "Oh no! How much did she hear?" he asked.

"Forget about her. She's got her own problems. Listen to me, Riley. There is always a choice, okay? Using that paper isn't the answer. Ask Madame Gaudette if you can hand in your own paper later. Take a penalty. Just do NOT hand in that one. Okay? Look, I have to go, but we'll figure out something later." Beth smiled gently and disappeared down the hallway.

Riley took a deep breath. He pulled out his essay and slowly approached Madame Gaudette's desk.

The only thing he could see was Lulu smiling at him. Everything else was a blur.

chapter 19

nowhere to turn

Halfway through French class, Lulu approached Madame Gaudette's desk. Riley watched with horror as she whispered into the French teacher's ear. Madame Gaudette gave Lulu her full attention.

What is she saying? Is she ratting me out? Agh! There must be a way out of this! Riley thought. He panicked. He did not know what to do next.

By this time, Madame Gaudette was sorting through the stack of term papers on her desk. She pulled out one of them and set it aside. Lulu was smiling.

That's it. I'm doomed! Riley thought. He spent the rest of the class staring at the clock. When the bell rang, Riley jumped out of his chair. He bolted for the door. He only stopped when he heard Madame Gaudette call his name. Her voice sounded firm.

"Riley! I need to speak with you," she said.

Oh, no! Busted! he thought. A wave of panic washed over him. He was just moments away from freedom. For a split second he considered pretending that he had not heard her at all.

Then she spoke again. "Now!"

"Here it comes!" Riley said under his breath.

The French teacher was not smiling. The last student left the room, and Madame Gaudette rose. "Please sit down," she told him. She pointed to a desk directly in front of her. The teacher watched him carefully before she spoke. "Is there something you would like to explain?" She was holding the stack of term papers.

"About what?" he replied. He decided to try and play it cool.

"About your paper," she said.

Please let this be over soon, he prayed.

"I need you to give me an explanation. There seems to be a problem," she continued.

"A problem? Wha...what do you mean? I don't understand," he lied.

"Riley...I can't help you if you refuse to be honest with me."

"I didn't do anything wrong! It's all a mistake! I don't know what Lulu told you, but it's not true!" he blurted out. He was beginning to shake.

"What are you talking about?" she said.

Now Riley was confused. He wondered if he could have been wrong about Lulu. "What did Lulu tell you about my essay?" he asked.

"Lulu? She did not say a thing about you. Though she did have some concerns about her own paper. I pulled it aside for her. That's how I found out that you had not handed in yours," she said.

"What do you mean?" Riley asked.

"I want to know what happened to your term paper. It isn't in this pile with the others. Yet, you were in the line of students handing in essays. Is there something wrong? This is a major paper. It is not like you to be late."

Wow. Lulu didn't say a thing about me, Riley thought to himself.

He studied Madame Gaudette. He did not know how to explain the last twenty-four hours to her. Maybe he could just show her. He reached into his backpack and pulled out the Internet essay. Just as Madame Gaudette reached for it, Riley paused and pulled it back. Her empty hand seemed frozen in midair.

Riley could not go through with it. "No. That's not it," he said after a pause. He searched through his bag and pulled out another one. *"This* is my paper." He passed it to her for real this time.

Riley looked up at the ceiling, down at the floor, and out the window. He looked anywhere except at the teacher. She stopped reading and looked up at Riley in confusion. "Is this it?"

Riley nodded and then looked at his feet. It was too painful to look her in the eye.

She looked puzzled. "Riley? First of all, it is not written in French. Second, these are only your research notes. There is no essay or author write-up here!"

Riley put his head down on the desk. How had his life become so out of control?

Madame Gaudette walked over to Riley. "Look, Riley. You are one of my top students. That is, you *were* one of my top students. Lately, however, your grades have been slipping. I'm concerned. This is not like your normal work. Why would you hand in something that is incomplete?" she asked.

He answered her in a quiet, slow voice. "Well, at least it's mine."

Madame Gaudette studied him. Then she spoke. "As I said earlier, I still don't have your essay," Madame Gaudette said. "I deduct a grade point each day an assignment is late.

Today you may have had an 'A' paper. Tomorrow it will only be worth 'A-.'" By this time, she was sitting back at her desk.

Riley thought about it. "By the time I finish, my paper will only be worth a 'C' if I'm lucky. There's not enough time to get a good mark. What's the point? I won't even have a chance at the Paris trip."

"Well, then. You shouldn't be wasting your time sitting here and making excuses with me. Good day, Riley. I'll see you in class tomorrow."

chapter 20

smell the fear

For the next week, Riley pulled late nights just to finish his essay for French class. It was his *own* paper this time. In the mornings he had to drag himself to school. Beth even found him sleeping in the library one day.

Now that the essay was finished, Riley could relax. He beamed as he munched one of Lee's famous onion rings.

"I never would have believed it. Getting a low grade can feel great!" He held up the French essay. There was a big, fat "C" at the top. He leaned back in the wooden booth at Lee's.

Beth agreed. "Who said that a low grade couldn't be sweet!"

"Yup! And I earned it all myself! This certainly is a beautiful day!" he grinned.

"*Mmmm*…sure…I guess it's as good as it's going to get for a report card day," Tyson said.

Riley stopped smiling. "Is that today? I almost forgot," he said in a grim voice. "My parents are in for a rude awakening. That French essay was worth fifty percent of my mark. I'm pretty sure I won't be going to Paris this summer. What am I going to tell my parents? *How* am I going to tell them?" Riley said.

"Well, the lying and cheating thing didn't work out for you. Maybe it's time to be honest with your parents," Beth offered.

"I wish I could be, but you know my parents," Riley said hopelessly.

"I can give you only one piece of advice. After you tell your parents…duck!" Tyson said.

"Ha. Ha. Very funny. I think I'd better go home and work out my defense plan. I'll see you guys tomorrow. I hope…" Riley said.

"Good luck!" Beth and Tyson said together.

As soon as he got home, Riley checked the mailbox. There it was—his report card. He pulled out the large, brown envelope stuffed inside. "There you are," he said to the envelope. "I can't believe how much grief you are about to cause." He ripped it open and read over his grades. "Hey! An 'A+' in photography! Great! History, 'B+,' not bad. Chemistry a 'B,' not so good. Uh oh…'C+' in French. Well…the bad news is that it won't get me to Paris. But the good news is that after my parents see this, they may boot me there. I may see Paris after all!" He said with a big sigh.

The light on the answering machine was flashing. The message was from his parents.

"Hello, Riley! Your father and I will be home early tonight. We want to celebrate your report card. How does dinner at *Chez Phillipe* sound to you? Who knows, maybe the next French meal you eat will be in Paris this summer! *Au revoir!*"

Riley began to feel sick. His parents were not going to take the news well. *There has got to be something I can do to fix this*, he thought.

Riley ran upstairs and turned on his computer. He would give one last effort to save his hide. Riley thought that maybe he could change the grades before his parents saw them. He figured that he could still pull up his grades before the end of the year. Forging his report card right now may not seem like such a big deal later.

He hurried to recreate his report card. His parents' car pulled into the driveway while he worked. Riley looked at his watch with panic. *It figures. The one day I want them to be late, they are actually home on time!* His chest tightened. There was that queasy feeling in his stomach again. He tried to ignore it.

There's no way I can do this. If I give them the fake report card, I'll be dead. If I give them the real one, I'll still be dead. He heard footsteps outside his bedroom. Riley turned the report cards over on his desk just as his parents came in.

Riley's father beamed. "Show us the good news! Where's your report card?"

"Uh, it's not here yet," Riley lied.

"Oh, really?" his mother said. "I called the school this morning. The office told me that we may be receiving them today. I know. I shouldn't be checking up, but who wants to wait for good news?"

His father leaned against the desk. Two pieces of paper floated to the floor. Riley made a grab for them, but it was too late. Mr. Jackson bent to pick them up.

"Riley? I thought you said that the reports weren't ready. Why am I holding a copy of your marks?" he asked. "Why am I holding *two* copies of your marks?" He read them over. Then he handed the papers to his wife. His face was turning purple.

Mrs. Jackson read over the two pieces of paper. She frowned. Without a word she handed both papers back to her husband.

Riley cringed at what was coming next. "I can explain—" he began.

Mr. Jackson cut him off and started to roar. "YOU CAN EXPLAIN *WHY* YOUR MARKS ARE SO LOW? YOU CAN EXPLAIN *WHY* YOU HAVE A FALSE REPORT CARD? YOU CAN EXPLAIN *WHY* YOU LIED ABOUT IT!"

"Well…you see…I've been under a lot of pressure this term," Riley said.

His mother looked at him with great disappointment. "Pressure? You have always handled pressure in the past, Riley. You will have to do better than that."

"I knew you guys wouldn't understand. You never really listen to me," Riley said.

"So, you figured that lying would make us pay attention?" Mr. Jackson said. His voice was still raised, but at least he was not yelling at Riley anymore.

His mother stepped in. "Adam, please! Stop overreacting. You're not helping the matter at all." Then she turned back to her son. "Go on, Riley. We're listening."

Riley grew hopeful. It sounded like they were going to listen. He took a deep breath and tried to explain.

"Well…it's just that there has been *more* pressure this year than I'm used to. Between my schoolwork, assignments, and darkroom time, there has been a lot more to do. Oh, right, I started a job, too."

Mr. and Mrs. Jackson stared at each other. "A JOB?" they said together.

"You know that we wanted you to focus on your grades," his father said.

"I shouldn't have lied, Mom. I'm sorry. But, I'm not so sure what I want to do anymore. No...that's not right." Riley paused and took a deep breath. He was nervous, but he had to tell them. "Mom. Dad. I think I want to be a photographer," he said.

Mr. Jackson shook his head. "Are you out of your mind? Do you know how hard your mother and I have worked to save for your education?" Before Riley could respond, Mr. Jackson turned to his wife. "Erika, hand me your cell phone, please. I'm going to call the Royal Academy. Maybe we can get our son in there. *We* are going to pull up those grades. Riley needs to learn how to get serious and focus on his future!" He stormed out of the room, phone in hand.

Riley knew about the Royal Academy. It was an all-boys school out east. It was supposed to be hard. School started at eight o'clock. Some courses did not finish until nine o'clock at night.

The teachers were tough, and they gave out a ton of homework. There would be no spare time to relax. When would he be able to take pictures? He did not want to be hundreds of miles away from his friends, either.

"There. It's all been arranged," Mr. Jackson said as he came back into the room. "We have an interview at the Academy next week. Until then, you are grounded. You can use your spare time to focus on your grades. Do you hear me, Riley?" his father said firmly.

"Yes, sir. I heard you…but I don't want to go," Riley answered. His voice was shaking. He had never stood up to his father like that. It felt scary, but he was not ready to give in.

"This is not about what you *want*, Son. We are in this mess because of what you thought you wanted," said his father.

"Riley, I know this may seem drastic. We really are doing this because it is what is best for you," she said.

"I'm not going!" Riley said firmly.

His father turned and glared at him. "What did you say, Son?"

Now Riley began to raise his voice. "Weren't you listening to me? I AM NOT GOING!" Riley stormed out of his room. He ran down the stairs, and slammed the front door behind him.

chapter 21

the trouble
with parents

Riley drove around for over an hour. He stopped at Riverside Park. He just had to get out and burn off the tension. He started to run. By the time he reached the railroad tracks he was panting. He had to slow down and stretch out the pain that burned in his side.

The moon peeked from beyond the clouds from time to time. The rest of the time he walked in almost complete darkness.

It's a good thing I'm really mad, or I'd be scared to death, he thought.

Riley kept trying to make sense of what had happened at home. He knew one thing for sure—he was *not* going away to boarding school. First he had to figure out where he was going to go that night. Staying at Tyson's was out of the question. Tyson's parents would try to convince him that he should go back home. They would want him to work things out with his parents. He was pretty sure that Beth would try to make him go home, too.

The clouds parted at last, and the moon shone through. Riley could see something ahead on the tracks. Actually, it was *someone*—a girl— but she had her back to him. Riley thought she would turn around as he approached, but she just faced the other way.

"Excuse me!" Riley said as he was about to pass her. The girl did not budge. She kept her chin tucked into her knees, and Riley could not see her face. He could hear her singing, though. The moonlight shone on her headphones. The volume was so loud that he could hear the music now, too. *No wonder she can't hear me!* He moved around her and kept walking down the railroad tracks.

After a few minutes, he thought he heard a train whistle. He looked over his shoulder. The lights of the late-night express train shone in the distance. The girl was far behind him. She still had not moved. Riley could not figure out what she was doing. She was just sitting there.

He tried shouting at her from a distance. That did not work. Riley turned back and walked quickly toward her. "HEY! A TRAIN IS COMING!" he yelled at her.

She still did not look up. The train was coming closer and was moving quickly now. Riley grew nervous. He picked up his pace and began to jog. He waved his arms to get her attention. The train had rounded the bend. The light shone down the tracks and straight into his eyes. The girl looked like a shadow as the light grew larger and brighter behind her. He could barely make her out.

His jog turned into a run. The whistle was blaring. *She must hear it now! Why isn't she moving? What if I can't make it in time?*

The train was almost upon them, and the whistle screeched for them to move. Riley was sure that the train would kill them both. He took a flying leap and knocked the girl off the tracks. The sound of their screams was drowned out by the train roaring by. Riley was deafened by the thundering noise of the great machine.

Riley was panting, and his face was covered in sweat. He looked over at the girl lying nearby him on the grass. It was Lulu Fontaine!

"Lulu! What are you doing out here?"

Lulu said nothing.

"You could have been killed! *We* could have been killed!" Riley shouted at her.

Lulu looked at him with contempt. "You should add 'young lady' to the end of that sentence. Then you would sound like my dad."

Riley stopped. He had the same out-of-control voice his father had used on him earlier. Now Riley looked carefully at Lulu. Her cheeks were stained with tears. Her hazel eyes were red and puffy. She had been crying—a lot.

"Lulu, what's wrong?" This time Riley asked her with true concern.

Lulu only stared at him.

"Listen, maybe I'm the last person in the world that you would want to talk to. Hey, I don't blame you. But your day couldn't have been as bad as mine. I guess you could say that I've had one 'lulu' of a day," Riley said. He gave her a half-smile.

Lulu scowled at his little joke. "What is your problem? Poor Riley didn't get all 'As' on his report card for a change?" she said.

"Actually...I didn't. I got a 'C+' in French class," he admitted.

Lulu looked stunned. "Ouch! What did your parents say?"

"For starters, they totally freaked out. Now they are planning to send me away to boarding school. They want to make sure that I will 'focus on my future,'" he told her.

"Wow! Are you sure we don't have the same parents?" she said with a small smile.

"Yours are pretty tough, too?" he asked.

Lulu nodded. "Yeah. Lately it's been worse since they've been going through the divorce. The only thing that stops them from yelling and insulting each other is me. The better I do at school, the more they forget that they hate each other," she told him.

Neither of them knew what to say next.

Finally, Riley took a chance. "Okay. I understand that things are pretty rough at home. Are things so bad that you are alone at the railroad tracks at night?"

"Well, *you're* out here on the railroad tracks—alone and at night," she said.

Riley grew quiet. "I see what you mean. But I tried to get you off the tracks. Did you really want to stay there?"

"No. It's not like that. I just came out here to think. I was tired, so I sat down for a bit." Lulu was silent again. "Riley, I know it's none of my business. How could you only got a 'C+' in French?" she asked quietly.

"At the start of the year, everything seemed okay. I had things under control. But then things just didn't feel right for *me* anymore," he said. "When I did find something that *I* liked, nothing else seemed that important. There was no way to explain that to my parents, though. They just want me to do what they say. Do you know what I mean?"

"Totally!" Lulu said. She seemed relieved. Her words began to tumble out. "When I think of all the late nights I've spent, I can't believe it. Then there has been all the pressure to keep up my marks. It's all been to make my parents happy. I mean...I *want* to do well in school. I know I'm smart. I'm just tired of trying to be the best all the time," she told him.

Riley agreed. "So what are we going to do now?" he asked.

They looked at each other. A strange thing happened. Riley almost liked Lulu now. In fact, he thought she felt the same way about him.

"Well, we can't run away," she said, looking him in the eye.

"We can't sit on the tracks and wait for the next train," he told her. He held out his hand.

Lulu took it and pulled herself up. "It looks like we'll have to stand our ground," she said.

"Yup. Even if it hurts us," Riley answered.

"Or our parents!" she laughed.

chapter 22

Riley Jackson: king of the world

It was one-thirty in the morning when Riley walked through the back door. He did not expect to see a crowd. Tyson, Beth, and his parents were sitting at the kitchen table. "Hello?" Riley said.

The group of people all turned their heads at once. "RILEY!" they cried. His mother dropped her cup in shock. Hot coffee spilled all over the white tile floor.

"I'm so glad you're okay," Beth said. She hurried over and hugged him tightly.

Riley did not want to let go. "I'm glad that you're here," he whispered in her ear. Riley gently pulled away. He gave Beth a warm smile.

Then his father stood up. Riley froze. Mr. Jackson grabbed Riley by the shoulders. Riley braced himself for what was going to come next. Before he knew it, his father was giving him a huge bear hug.

"I'm glad you're home, Son," said his father. There were tears in his eyes.

Riley was stunned. He could only think of a few times in his life when his father had hugged him. This time it had nothing to do with school. His dad was happy just to see *him*.

"Thanks, Dad," Riley said with relief. "I thought you would still be mad at me."

Mrs. Jackson spoke. "You were so angry when you left, Riley. We had never seen you act like that before. Your father and I were surprised, to say the least. When you didn't come home, we called Tyson and Beth. They hadn't heard from you either. It wasn't like you not to call. We were worried—and scared."

"Of course you didn't think that I would ever act that way. You guys never really listen to me. You're always talking *at* me and telling me what I should do next. You never seem to bother to ask me what I want," Riley said quietly.

Mrs. Jackson shook her head. "That's not true, Riley. We talk all the time."

"By phone messages, maybe," Riley said.

His father spoke. "Look Son, we understand that you don't want to go to the Academy. You have to understand that we have thought a lot about your future. We have more life experience than you do. Trust us on this." He looked over at his wife. "Isn't that right, Erika?"

Mrs. Jackson paused. "I'm not so sure anymore. Maybe he should stay here. Perhaps photography would be a good thing. He really does seem focused, Adam. We have always encouraged Riley to go after his goals," she said.

Mr. Jackson turned to his wife in disbelief. "What are you talking about, Erika? Riley is a gifted student. I don't want to see him wasting his brain on taking pictures."

Mrs. Jackson glared at her husband. "I didn't realize that you felt that way about photography," she said. Her voice was strained. She pushed back her chair and went upstairs. A few minutes later she returned, carrying a large black scrapbook. Mrs. Jackson handed it to her son. "Here, Riley. I think it's time you saw this." She gave him a soft smile.

Riley looked at each of his parents. He had no idea what was going on. Riley opened the album. Dozens of black and white photographs filled the pages. "What is this?" Riley asked.

In a quiet voice, his father answered him. "That belongs to your mother. Those are her photographs," Mr. Jackson said.

"Did you take all of these pictures?" Riley said to her.

"I did," his mother answered.

Riley was speechless. Tyson looked over Riley's shoulder as he turned the pages of his mother's album.

"You were a photographer?" Beth asked.

"I *was*," Riley's mother said.

"Your mother majored in art at university during her first year," said Mr. Jackson.

"You did?" Riley said.

His mother took a deep breath and began. "Believe it or not, I did. That was before I entered law school. I took photography. Actually, I was pretty good at it."

"You were great at it, Erika," Mr. Jackson said softly. He sat down beside Riley and pulled the scrapbook toward him. Riley's father started to look through the pages, too. "Your mother won an award for that one," he said. He pointed to a picture of a runner. She was breaking through a ribbon at the finish line. Her face was twisted in pain. Yet she had a look of joy in her eyes. "It's a powerful picture," he said quietly.

"So, if you were that good at it, why didn't you stay with it? Why did you become a lawyer?" Riley asked. "That seems like a pretty big change to make."

"My parents didn't approve of my choices. They would not pay for my schooling if I studied art. I wanted to go to school. I just couldn't afford it on my own. After a lot of arguing, I agreed to go into law. Luckily, I found a love for it, too. I like helping people," she explained. "Besides, if I hadn't gone to law school, then I may not have met your father. There he is," she said. Mrs. Jackson pointed to a younger picture of her husband.

Riley, Tyson, and Beth crowded to see.

"You were cute, Mr. Jackson!" Beth said.

"Yeah! You've got a lot more hair there, sir!" Tyson said. He patted him on the back.

"Easy, now!" Mr. Jackson smiled.

"But Mom, you would never give up like that now. I don't understand. Your pictures are really good," Riley said.

Mrs. Jackson grew silent. She and her husband looked at each other for a long time. Then his mother spoke again. "We will understand if you don't want to go to boarding school. It's okay if you want to do something else. Take some time to find out if you really want to take pictures," said Mrs. Jackson.

"Really?" Riley said. Riley looked at his father, who was nodding in agreement with his wife. "Oh, man! Thank you!"

Tyson and Beth both breathed a sigh of relief. It could have turned out a lot worse.

"Wait a minute," his mother said. "I'm not finished. You are not off the hook. There still is the matter of your grades to deal with. And I'm not sure what to do about the lying."

"I really am sorry about all the lying. I don't know what else to say. But I do know that I won't act that way again," he promised.

"I think that summer school will be appropriate. You won't be able to make that Paris trip, Son," his father said.

Riley looked down. "I think that my C+ pretty much gave it away," he said. "Lulu Fontaine will probably go."

"Sorry," Tyson said in sympathy.

"No. It's okay," Riley said with a secret smile. "Lulu deserves it."

"Wow. What happened to you today? Were you struck by lightning or something?" Tyson said with disbelief.

"Something like that," Riley said.

"It's too bad about Paris, Riley. But then again, there is always summer with your friends. I have a feeling it's going to be better than ever," Beth said. She gave him promising wink and reached for his hand.

Riley squeezed it tightly.

Tyson gave a large sigh. *"Ahhh!"* Then he stared at the ceiling for a moment. He seemed to be deep in thought.

Uh oh, thought Riley. *Here comes another one of his plans.*

"Hmmm. Maybe you'll be lucky enough to see the lovely Willow Thomson," said Tyson.

"Oh, Willow? We're old friends now. Maybe I *could* be persuaded to put in a good word for you. In fact, I think you should give her a call yourself. That is, if you aren't afraid of a pretty girl," Riley said.

"Who me? Um…of course I'm not afraid. You know how I am with the ladies," Tyson said. He almost looked a bit shy.

"Riiiight…" Riley laughed.

Riley looked up and caught Beth's eye. They both smiled a private smile. The future was looking very good indeed.

glossary

au revoir
A French phrase that means "good-bye"

bien sûr
A French phrase that means "of course"

binoculars
A handheld tool that is used to look at objects that are far away

bonjour
A French word that means "hello"

classe
A French word that means "class"

La Sorbonne
A university in Paris, France

Le Louvre
A famous art gallery in Paris, France

negative
A piece of camera film that has been soaked in chemicals. It holds images that are used to create photographs.

oui
A French word that means "yes"

pardonnez-moi
A French phrase that means "pardon me"

plagiarism
The act of taking someone else's thoughts
or ideas and using them as your own

police bust
A slang term that refers to a raid or an arrest

portfolio
A collection of photographs

professional
Describing a person who has a job or career

Single Lens Reflex (SLR) camera
A type of camera used by professional
photographers. To take a picture, light passes
through a single lens. This light bounces off a
mirror inside the camera.

The Three Musketeers
A novel by Alexandre Dumas that takes place
during the 17th Century. In it, three young men
set off on a daring adventure across France.

tripod
A camera stand with three legs